1093

Hot Spr and Bears

Lee Aucoin, *Creative Director*
Jamey Acosta, *Senior Editor*
Heidi Fiedler, *Editor*
Produced and designed by
Denise Ryan & Associates
Illustration © Bill Bolton
Rachelle Cracchiolo, *Publisher*

Teacher Created Materials
5301 Oceanus Drive
Huntington Beach, CA 92649-1030
http://www.tcmpub.com
Paperback: ISBN: 978-1-4333-5637-7
Library Binding: ISBN: 978-1-4807-1736-7
© 2014 Teacher Created Materials

Written by
Nicolas Brasch

Illustrated by
Bill Bolton

Contents

Chapter One

The
Competition

Sai saw the letter on the kitchen table when she got home from school. It was addressed to her.

Sai Chandra
356 Fern Drive
Brooks, ME
       04921

TOY STORE GIVEAWAY!
WRITE AND WIN

Write a poem about your new toy. You could win a trip for your family to any place in the world!

Five hundred runners-up will receive $20 gift cards.

Poems cannot be longer than 35 words.

She looked at the back.

Pa's Plush Toys
4856 Valley Road
Burbank, CA
91508

Sai's heart started racing. She had entered a contest after she had bought a teddy bear from the toy store. The bear had come with an entry form for the contest.

Sai had spent days writing and re-writing her poem until she was completely happy with it. As Sai opened the envelope, she started thinking, *What if I won? I could go anywhere in the world!* She quickly got rid of the thought. *That's impossible!* But maybe she could start thinking about what she could buy with a $20 gift card!

Inside the envelope was a letter.

Dear Sai,

I am pleased to tell you that you have won The Pa's Plush Toys Poetry Contest. You and your family can choose to go anywhere in the world for a two-week vacation.

That was as far as Sai read. She raced into the living room, squealing with delight. Her dad and younger brother Ben could hardly believe the news.

Chapter Two

So Many Choices

Once they had gotten over the shock, Sai and her family started thinking about where to take their vacation. They looked online. They looked at books.

They spun their globe around and around. Where would they go?

Everyone agreed it should be Sai's choice, as she had won the contest, but they also agreed Dad and Ben each could make one suggestion.

"Chile would be amazing," said Sai's dad. "I've always wanted to explore volcanoes, and Chile is full of volcanoes." Sai agreed exploring volcanoes sounded like a lot of fun.

"I vote Canada," said Ben. "I want to get close to a brown bear. I think they're the coolest animals in the world." Sai agreed it would be fun to see a brown bear up close.

"I'd like to go to New Zealand," said Sai. "It has hot springs. I think playing in hot springs sounds like a lot of fun. Let me think about it. All our ideas sound great!"

Sai spent most of the next day doing more research for the trip. This was a decision she wanted to get right.

The next evening, the family got together in the living room. They waited for Sai to announce her choice.

"We're going somewhere you can explore volcanoes," Sai told them.

"Chile!" her dad yelled with excitement.

"No, not Chile."

"We're going somewhere you can get close to brown bears," Sai told them.

"Canada!" Ben yelled.

"No, not Canada."

"We're going somewhere we can bathe in hot springs," Sai told them.

"New Zealand?" asked Dad.

"No, not New Zealand."

"So where *are* we going?" Dad asked.

Sai took a deep breath, smiled, and said, "Kamchatka!"

"*Where?*" Dad and Ben asked together.

Chapter Four

Up, Up, and Away

Sai showed them where Kamchatka was on a map. But the map didn't reveal much about where they would be going. All it showed was a peninsula in northeastern Russia, near the Pacific Ocean.

Sai's family had to catch a plane from Maine to Alaska. Then, they caught another plane from Alaska to Kamchatka. When they finally arrived in Kamchatka, it was early in the morning and ten degrees.

"This is going to be a cold trip," moaned Ben.

"And it's summer time," laughed Sai.

Sai's family stayed in a hotel at the foot of a volcano. Rows and rows of volcanoes could be seen in the distance. They seemed to be surrounded by volcanoes.

"This peninsula is part of the Pacific Ring of Fire," Sai explained.

"What's that?" asked Ben.

"It's an area around the Pacific Ocean where there are hundreds of volcanoes."

"Not all of them erupt," Dad added quickly, in case Ben was feeling scared. But rather than being scared, Ben was excited.

The next day, a guide drove the family to the base of a huge volcano. There was no way they could climb to the top, since it was over eleven-thousand feet high—and covered in snow. Dad took some photos of the volcano's deep ravines. Over the next few days, they explored more than fifteen volcanoes.

As they lay in bed one night, they could hear one of the volcanoes rumbling. The next morning, smoke was billowing from a vent.

One day, the guide took them over two active volcanoes in a helicopter. Sai, Ben, and Dad were thrilled by the sight. "I wonder if Chile is like this," said Sai's dad.

Chapter Five

Hot Springs and Brown Bears

"Today, it's time for another treat," said Sai. But she wouldn't tell Ben and Dad what it was.

She secretly put everyone's swimsuits in her backpack. The guide drove the family to a river, which ran through a valley. All around was snow and ice. The river looked like it was covered with a layer of smoke. As they walked closer, they realized it wasn't smoke, but steam. For the rest of the day, they swam and played in the hot, bubbling water.

"I wonder if New Zealand is like this," mused Sai.

They had had so many adventures, but now it was nearing the end of their vacation. Ben was unusually quiet. He wouldn't tell anyone what was wrong. But Sai knew.

"There's just one more thing we have to see," said Sai. She led them toward the car waiting outside their hotel. The car took them to the airport, where a helicopter was waiting. The pilot held the door open for them, and they climbed in eagerly.

"Look, a bear!" yelled Ben as the helicopter reached a large nature reserve. "And look, there's another one! And over there! They're everywhere!"

"There's a cub!" shrieked Sai.

The pilot took them as close as he could without disturbing the bears. For Ben, it was like a dream come true. There were hundreds of huge brown bears in the reserve.

"I wonder if Canada is like this," said Ben.

"You know, I think Kamchatka is like nowhere else in the world," Sai replied. Dad and Ben nodded in agreement. This was a vaction they would never forget.

Nicolas Brasch lives in Melbourne, Australia. He writes both fiction and nonfiction books for children. Several of his books have won Australian Educational Publishing Awards, and in 2011, his book *Theme Parks, Playgrounds, and Toys* was shortlisted in the Australian Children's Book Council Awards. Nicolas also wrote *The Baseball Giant* for Read! Explore! Imagine! Fiction Readers.

Bill Bolton lives in Nottingham, England. Before Bill began illustrating children's books, he spent many years working for two major greeting card publishers. He loves developing new characters, and he works both traditionally with a paintbrush and electronically with a computer mouse. *Hot Springs and Brown Bears* is Bill's first book for Read! Explore! Imagine! Fiction Readers.